HOT ROMANCE
Breaking the Bonds

JACK RYDER

WARNING

This book contains sexually explicit scenes and adult language. It may be considered offensive to some readers. This book is for sale to adults ONLY.

* * * * * * * * * * * * * * * * * * *

Please store your files wisely where they cannot be accessed by underage readers.

Please feel free to send me an email. Just know that these emails are filtered by my publisher. Good news is always welcome.

Jack Ryder - **jack_ryder@awesomeauthors.org**

About the Publisher

4Fun Publishing, a member of **BLVNP Incorporated**, 340 S. Lemon #6200, Walnut CA 91789, info@blvnp.com / legal@blvnp.com
NOTE: Due to the highly emotional reaction of some people to works of erotic fiction, any email sent to the above address that contains foul language or religious references is automatically deleted by our anti-spam software and will not be seen. All other communications are welcome.

DISCLAIMER

Please don't be stupid and kill yourself. This book is a work of FICTION. Do not try any new sexual practice that you find in this book. It is fiction and not to be confused with reality. Neither the author nor the publisher or its associates assume any responsibility for any loss, injury, death or legal consequences resulting from acting on the contents in this book. Every character in this book is over 18 years of age. The author's opinions are not to be construed as the opinions of the publisher. The material in this book is for entertainment purposes ONLY. Enjoy.

Breaking the Bonds
Hot Romance

By: Jack Ryder

© Jack Ryder 2014
ISBN: 978-1-62761-735-2

Chapter One

I have been at odds with my father for as long as I can remember. As with many rich and powerful men, he tends to treat his family the same way he has made millions: By being a very ruthless bully. My father does not accept no for an answer under any circumstance. He has no respect for any opinion other than his own. He trusts no one and he takes a perverse joy in imposing his will on everyone involved with him.

My first vivid memory of my father happened when I was five years old. I had received a brand new bicycle for my birthday from my Mother. After two days of riding it around the front of our estate with training wheels, I was just beginning to feel a little bit of confidence. That was when my dear father decided I should be a man.

After he removed the training wheels, he ordered me to climb on. With tears in my eyes I begged him to not make me do this. He placed one hand on my back and the other on one of the handlebars. As he began to push me down the driveway, he barked "Don't you dare let me down, son!"

I made it about thirty feet after he let go of me and the bike. I had steadily gained speed as I wobbled down the driveway. The pedals were now moving so fast my little feet could not keep up as the handle bars wiggled so hard that I could no longer hold on. The front wheel finally made a sudden jerk to the left and I was thrown head first onto the pavement.

As I laid there bleeding from a gash on the top of my head, he stood over me and screamed at me to stop crying like a sissy. He pulled me up off the pavement by the arm and shouted at me that he had not given me permission to stop riding the bike. He shouted that he would not have a son who was too stupid to ride a bike. When he finally realized that the bike had been too damaged to force me to get back on, he told me to have mom tend to my injury. He instructed his body guard to throw away my bicycle. He never mentioned the incident again.

I FIRST met Dad's new wife Mandy last year when I came home for spring break from college. It was my last year and I would be graduating with honors by the start of summer. I decided to not go party with my friends so I could finish writing my Master Thesis. I knew at the estate I would have plenty of privacy and silence.

Even when my father is at home I rarely see him because the estate is so massive and I purposely stay to the rear most wing of the estate. That location also has the benefit of overlooking the Olympic-sized pool, double-sized tennis court and cabana style sauna rooms that are behind the estate. That was where I first saw Mandy.

I had pretty much finished up my thesis and was mostly just finishing the reference entries.

I decided to take a break and take a dip in the pool. As I glanced out the back window, there she was, laying on one of the chaise lounge chairs. Her golden dark tanned skin made the tiny white bikini seem even more sensual somehow. She had a hint of a smile on her face as she glanced up at me in the window.

I felt a little embarrassed as I realized that I was becoming erect as I stared down at her. Her tiny little white bikini did little to conceal her bombshell figure. The tiny triangles on top covered maybe one third of her 36C cone shaped jugs and the one between her legs barely covered her pussy. Even from a hundred feet away, I could plainly see that her nipples were fully erect and pressed tightly against the flimsy fabric.

I nearly decided not to go down to the pool that day. I felt really weird about lusting after my father's new wife. I felt foolish that I would desire anything that belonged to him. And make no mistake, she belonged to him. But it was such a beautiful warm sunny day that I really did want to go do some laps in the pool. All of the sitting around writing for the last several months had me desperate to do something physical. And swimming has always been my exercise of choice.

"I was wondering if you would have the nerve to come down," she taunted me as I made my approach. She did nothing to attempt to conceal the camel toe between her legs or the fact that I could clearly see half of both her coral pink areolas. "I guess your father was wrong about you." She said it softly as she glanced up and down my body. "I don't see anything spineless about you at all." She said it in a giggly suggestive sort of way.

I felt a sudden contempt that her words had pressed a button inside but was relieved that the wiggle that had started in my swim trunks went away as the blood rushed to my face from my anger. "Would you be a dear and oil me up?" she reached over to hand me a large bottle of tanning oil. "I'm sure your father won't object." He voice sounded almost secretive. "He probably thinks you are the only man on Earth that he has nothing to fear about."

As she rolled over onto her stomach, one of her tits popped out of the top. I got a very good glance at her soft luscious globe before she tucked it back inside. "Oops...silly me!" she giggled in a naughty tone of voice. Her bikini bottom was tightly wedged into the crack of her ass. I was feeling even more anger after her last remark about my father's feelings towards me.

I poured nearly half the bottle of oil all over her back and ass. The oil quickly soaked through the flimsy white fabric of her suit bottoms. It made the fabric completely transparent. I could now see every inch of her gorgeous tight ass. "Oops...silly me!" I taunted her back playfully. I very roughly rubbed the oil all over her back, legs and thighs. I made it a point to not make it a very pleasurable experience. Part of that was to keep me from growing another boner. But I also wanted her to know that I was not pleased with her.

I took one last glance at her gorgeous round ass then slapped her hard on her left buttock. "All done!" I growled. Then I ran off and jumped into the pool. I was happy to be in the cool soothing water. Not only had the anger remained in my face, but I had begun to grow another boner as I rubbed the oil all over her silky smooth body. I had made it a point to keep my hands away from her inner thighs and gorgeous ass. But the transparency of her oil-soaked bikini had made it impossible for me to not stare at her perfect round bottom.

I had just finished my 30th lap in the 25-yard long pool and decided to call it good. As I pulled myself up along the side of the pool, I happened to glance over to the cabana nearest to the pool.

Mandy was just inside showering in the nude. The door was wide open. "Oooh Geeezus, look at that," I whispered to myself.

From behind, the lily white triangle on her ass from her tan line was very arousing to me. With her skin a deep golden brown, the whiteness on her ass was electrifying. She was bent over and my mind raced with thoughts of mounting that sweet white ass from behind. I had frozen in my tracks and now my cock was fully erect.

Without warning, she stood up and turned towards me. The white triangles on her breasts and between her legs were even more sensual to me. "Oh God!" I think I said it a little louder than I intended. I could feel my cock pounding inside my swimming trunks as she glanced up at me.

I was still frozen. Unable to make myself look away, Mandy moved to the door and just stood there for a few moments smiling at me. Then she closed the door.

I remained motionless for several more moments with the vision of her nakedness seared into my brain. Then I made a dash for the house and ran up the stairs two at a time. I quickly undressed and jumped into my huge walk in shower with the nozzles that spray you from every angle. I closed my eyes and envisioned her gorgeous nude body as I slowly began to stroke my cock.

It felt a little funny to me at first. It has been many years since I saw a woman that I felt like fantasizing over, or felt this desperate to masturbate. With the money that my father has channeled into my account along with the funds I earn on my own, I have enough money to have any woman I desire and usually take full advantage of that.

I could clearly see her in my mind's eye. The sexy white triangle pointing down to her bare slit with just one little patch of blond pubic hair carefully sculpted in the shape of a heart. Her full 36C cone-shaped tits with the lily white triangles. Her coral pink areolas and matching nipples that poked out at least an inch from the center. I could see her crystal sapphire blue eyes smiling at me and her pouty lips looking like they need to be wrapped around my prick.

I had been frantically jerking myself as I envisioned all of this. The thought of her luscious pouty lips engulfing my rigidness sent me over the edge. "Oh yes, Mandy…Oh Yes...Oh Yes," I was surprised that I had moaned it out loud. My cock sprayed three heavy wads of sperm all over the shower wall.

I sort of felt a little embarrassed inside as I rinsed myself off in the warm shower spray. It has been so long since I have masturbated that I sort of felt like a silly teenage school boy. "Damn you!" I wasn't sure if I was chastising her for flaunting her body so openly or at myself for wanting her so desperately. As I dried myself off, I reasoned with myself that this would not happen again. "That's Dad's property!" I reminded myself sternly.

Later in the afternoon, I received a call from my father on my cell phone. "Dinner will be at 6 pm sharp. Be there! I want to introduce my wife!" He said it in the familiar commanding voice. Before

I could tell him I had plans, which involved a cute little redhead I had just met, he hung up. It was clearly not negotiable. I found it curious that I suddenly found myself considering what I should wear. As if I need to look appealing to her. I definitely chose a pair of threadbare faded jeans and one of those flowery Hawaiian type shirts in a deep blue and white pattern.

I got there at five after six just to piss him off. "Sorry I'm late." I said it casually as if it was not big deal. "Had to cancel the dinner date I had planned!" It was my way of letting him know that he had interrupted my plans.

"This was HER request!" He said it gruffly. "Sit!" He really does love to hear the sound of his own voice. Especially if it is imposing his will on someone.

"This is Mandy." He pointed his fork at her as if she were just one of his toys. "She tells me you met briefly at the pool." As I reached for her hand, I wondered exactly how much she had told him. Did she mention that I had my hands all over her body? Had she mentioned that I had stared at her naked body for several long minutes? "It's a pleasure to meet you...formally," I told her as I kissed the back of her hand. "I'm Connor," I added more cheerfully than I planned.

I could feel the beginning of a wiggle between my legs as I sat down. The dress she was wearing was so very seductive. It was a white jersey style full length dress that clung to her body so perfectly that you could clearly see every inch of her curvy voluptuous body. I could clearly see the perfect shape of her cone shaped breasts and even could make out the diameter of her areolas pressed tightly into the fabric. It was also very low cut so there was lots of cleavage on display.

I did my best to keep my eyes off of her as we had our meal. When she made small talk so

I had to look at her. I kept my eyes glued to her sparkling blue eyes. I noticed that she glanced down several times as if to get me to look at her tits. But I kept myself focused and reminded myself that Penny, the little redhead, would be mine for the night as soon as this torture was over. I ate as quickly as I could without seeming like a starved longshoreman.

"You seem distracted, Connor," she whispered it in a giggle as my father became involved in an unexpected business call on his cell. She had removed her sandal and was now rubbing her foot up and down my thigh just inches from my prick. When I glanced down, I saw that she had pulled the bottom of her dress, which was slit all the way up one side to the hip, over to expose her bare pussy to me.

"I...have a date!" My reply almost sounded like a gasp. She smiled coyly as she pulled her dress back into place just as Dad ended his call. "Surely she can't be as fascinating company as we are!" her toes rubbed my rigid prick as she said it sweetly. "Maybe not...but then...I won't be sleeping with either of you tonight!" I said it as a taunt to both her and my father. He has never condoned my propensity for "sleeping around" as he puts it.

I was glad when my father announced that he had unexpected business to attend to and quickly left the table. That only left Mandy to gawk at the erection that was throbbing in my jeans when I got up to leave. "Ooooh look at that," Mandy giggled. "Did I do thaaaaat?" she smiled. "Nope!" I winked at her shrewdly. "I was just thinking of that little redhead waiting to spread her legs for me," I goaded her. "See ya!" I left her sitting there alone at the table.

I found myself thinking about Mandy as I made my drive to see Penny. She was so brazen, and what was she doing rubbing my prick with her foot with my father just a couple of feet away? Penny had been disappointed about the cancelled dinner date but had told me to save some room for dessert. "I'll have something special for you," she had told me. I tried to shake Mandy out of my brain as I pulled into the cono parkway.

When she opened the door, my teeth nearly dropped out of my mouth. My sexy little redhead was letting me know exactly what her intentions were! She was wearing a black see through baby doll nightie that was so short that it did not completely cover her pussy which was bare since she was not wearing panties.

My cock was already fully erect by the time I stepped inside and closed the door behind me.

As a true redhead, her milky white translucent skin glowed through the transparent black fabric and her 38DD jugs swayed as she led me to her couch. Her lily white ass swished back and forth as we walked. In my mind I could still envision Mandy bent over in that shower.

After Penny unbuttoned my shirt and removed it, she pushed me back until I was seated on the couch. "I think you are going to like this," she whispered as she removed my sandals and then my 501 jeans. After she sat down on my thighs with my rigid dick between her thighs, just inches from her sexhole, she reached back to the coffee table and picked up the can of whipped cream that was sitting there.

She then ripped her nightie open with her free hand and sprayed a large amount of the sweet thick cream all over her huge tits. "Dessert is served!" she proclaimed with a giggle.

As she bent forward to present her cream slathered tits to me, I could feel her pussy dripping onto my throbbing prick. "And what should we do with this?" she giggled as I began to hungrily lick the whipped cream from her huge 38DD breasts. I felt her hand move down between us and suddenly I felt the sloppy wetness of her cunt as she scooted forward to impale herself on my throbbing 9-inch pecker.

The slick sweetness of the cream was very erotic to me as she began to rock back and forth on my cock. I licked and slurped and sucked on both of her tits till I had swallowed all of the cream. As she began to savagely grind her pussy into me harder and harder, I twisted on one of her nipples while I gently bit down on the other. "Ooooh fuck yes...fuck yes," she moaned with a deep sultry gasp.

As I continued to maul her tits with my mouth and left hand, I reached around her hips with my other hand and began to run my finger up and down the crack of her ass. "Oh yes...Yes, do that, do thaaaaaat!" Her voice was a throaty moan. When I felt her body beginning to vibrate close to her climax, I shoved my middle finger up her ass as far as it would go. "OH FUCK YES! FUCK

YES!OH MY GOD...YES!

Her body was bucking on top of mine like a cowgirl in a rodeo as her pussy had spasm after climaxes rushing through her pussy. As my cock started to ejaculate deep into her drenched sexhole, I twisted cruelly on her left nipple as my semen flooded into her. At that moment I was thinking of Mandy's nipples and how I would love to twist them this hard. Penny wet herself and her piss flooded down my legs as I finally let go of her tit. "That was...fucking incredible!" Penny gasped.

I spent the night with Penny even though I most often prefer to sleep alone in my own bed. I really did not want to take the chance that I would run into Mandy if I went home. I made it a point to screw Penny again in the morning before I left. It had the benefit of providing the possibility for me to fuck Penny again in the future if I should so desire. It also emptied my balls so I would not be horny if I ran into Mandy while I was packing to go back to school.

"I have a thing for school boys!" Her voice was a seductively teasing tone. I looked up from my luggage laying on the bed and glanced over to the doorway where she was standing. Her little remark sort of pissed me off. Although I am still in college, I actually graduated a year before her but I had moved on to a Master's program rather than spreading my legs for a gravy train job.

Mandy was wearing a very short white satin robe. Although it was not transparent, it clung to her body and I could easily see the curvature of her wonderful tits pressed against the soft satin. It was open enough in the front that I could see nearly half of her jugs including some of the lily white triangles. It was also obvious that she was nude underneath the robe. "Then why did you marry a man 30 years older than you?" I shot back at her.

The coy little smile fell from her face and I noticed that she pulled her robe closed a little. There was a look on her face that seemed familiar to me somehow. "I just...wanted to.. say that...I was sorry that I upset you yesterday out at the pool." She whispered it as she took a couple of steps into the room. I was able to get little glances at her pussy with each step that she took.

"I should never have said those things that your father said about you." It almost sounded like her voice was trembling a little. "I know that he can be...very demanding...very forceful!" It was like she was choosing her words wisely. "He is a MEAN, SELF ABSORBED BULLY!" I shouted back. I was surprised at my vehemence.

When I shouted at her, she had jumped and her robe fell open, exposing her nakedness to me.

I stood there gawking at her for several moments and she just stared back. There was a look on her face that almost seemed hopeful. "I could make it up to you!" her eyes told me that she was serious about her offer. "Apology accepted," I whispered as I closed my luggage case and shut the clasps. "You don't have to fuck me. I'll never say a word to my Dad!" I pressed my way past her and nearly ran down the stairway. I was deeply afraid I would change my mind and throw her on the bed. That was what every fiber of my body wanted to do.

Chapter Two

In reality, I really did not need to go back for that last two months of school. It was really just a matter of turning in my thesis and then clearing out my belongings from the little apartment two blocks from the school that had been my home away from home for the last several years. But I wanted these last two months to myself to finish my newest project. Plus, I wanted the extra time to prepare myself for the firestorm that was going to happen when I tell my father that I will not be coming to work for him.

Just out of high school, my father had bullied me into choosing "Communications" as my major at the college. It was his intention that I become the voice of his company. I would be his personal press and yarn spinner. I would be his media contact and his PR agent. The idea being that as his son, I would always make him look good and sweep up all the messes of havoc that his self-interested belligerence so often creates.

My father had never bothered to notice that my real interest, my passion, was for writing. He dismissed my scholarship for English Literature as a kindness from the school in anticipation that he would contribute to their Alumni Scholarship Fund. He never bothered to think that maybe I had earned that award or to consider what I wanted to do with my life.

My mother left him the week after I went off to college. She knew what I wanted. She knew of my dreams. She knew how important it was to me. It was the final straw for her after 18 years of being bullied and manipulated by him. Because of her prenuptial agreement with him, he would not support her in any way after the divorce.

Wisely, she had squirreled away nearly half of the monthly allowance he gave her for over ten years. She had put it in a secret bank account out of his reach. She left with plenty of money to survive on for the rest of her life. I had learned a valuable lesson from my Mother as a result of all that. I have saved over 60 percent of my father's monthly deposits into my account. Two weeks ago I opened a separate protected Swiss account and deposited well over two million dollars in it.

There was one other reason for coming back for these last two months. Some of my classmates refer to it as the "Goodbye Syndrome". They informed me that during the last couple of months before graduation there is window of time when many of the girls that have been out of reach for some reason or other, suddenly decide to have a wild fling before they go on to the next step in their lives.

Although I had never had to go without a bedmate whenever I desired one, there were a couple girls that had once treated me as if I was not good enough for them since I did not hang out with their high society group. Although I don't have any hang-ups about being rich, I have never blended well with the nose-in-the-air snobs that tend to belong to those type groups.

After the success of my first project and it became common knowledge that I had made a name for myself and a ton of money, they had both suddenly sought me out and made it very plain that they would love to "spend some time alone" with me. I made up my mind that I would throw them a bone, so to speak. But my plan is to do them together, convince them to have sex with each other as well as with me.

I called them each that afternoon and arranged for them to meet me at the most posh hotel downtown at 9 pm. I suggested to each that they wear the sexiest lingerie that they own and cover it by wearing a trench coat and high heels. I knew that there was a possibility that one of them or even both might just leave. But that didn't really matter. Just getting them to show up would be making them eat their words. Plus, I figured that my newfound notoriety might just make them willing to go along with my kinky little experiment. They could be my first groupies.

I had started writing short Adult Erotic stories during my first year in college. It was my way of relaxing and escaping the drudgery of school studies and avoiding the infantile beer bust parties so common to all Universities these days. After I had posted over a hundred of them to an online site, I was invited by reputable publisher to submit some stories for them.

My first dozen Erotic Romances did marginally well and I was just beginning to earn an income from them. But the money was not the point. I LOVED writing and it thrilled me to see my stories in print. Each time I received an email from one of my readers, it made me feel happier inside than I had ever experienced.

Then, a year and a half ago, I had written my first novel. It was a Wizardry type story. But it was quite different than others that you would normally find. My story was basically an Adult Erotic Wizardry tale that was both highly entertaining and very sexually explicit. To my great surprise, it became a huge success. It sold over one million copies in the first year of print. When I was pressed to do book signing engagements, my identity was quickly known and I became an instant hero at the University.

Amy was the first to arrive. She looked thrilled when I answered the door wearing a robe that was identical to the Wizards Robe I had described in my book. I asked her in and handed her an autographed hardcover copy of the book. I opened it so she could read the inscription. *"Let us always remember our special time together...Love Connor"*

Amy shrieked as she read my words and jumped into my arms to give me a very passionate kiss. As she stepped back, I took the opportunity to remove her trench coat. "Oooh, look at you!" It was an honest gasp of pleasure. She was wearing a black transparent bra with matching transparent panties. She also had black silk stockings with a black garter belt with black heels. I led her quickly to the bed and sat her down at the foot of the bed just as there was a knock on the door. "There will be one more for our little party!" I announced softly.

Before she could reply, I quickly went to the door and let Susan in. If I could pull this off, it would give me great joy that I had convinced these two best friends to have sex with each other as well as with me. After I handed the autographed book and was again kissed passionately, I stripped her coat off and was thrilled that she was naked other than white transparent nylons held up by a white garter belt. "Oh Susan...Look at how lovely you are!" I crooned.

I dropped her coat on the floor next to Amy's and let her to the bed. There was a very long silence as they were now face to face practically in the nude. "You both look so beautiful together!" I said it softly as I gently turned Susan and again kissed her very passionately. She hesitated at first but soon began to return my passions vigorously. I allowed her to push my robe off so I would be completely exposed to the both of them.

"Oooh...Look at Thaaaaaat!" it was Amy who had moaned as she saw my throbbing 9-inch prick just inches from her face since she was still seated on the bed. I held my hand out to her and smiled. "Come join us, sweetheart," I whispered softly. She hesitated for just a moment until she saw Susan smile and nod her head. I was elated! This was going to work after all.

I had one on each side at first. I took turns kissing one and then the other. I pulled them closer and closer together so their faces were practically against each other as I kissed back and forth.

Then, I pushed them together so they were face to face. "Kiss each other for me," I said it very softly. "Show me how special your friendship is." They hesitated just for a moment, but then they were suddenly kissing one another hungrily. It was as if they have wanted to do this for a very long time.

I stepped back so I could enjoy watching them better. From this distance I could see both of their gorgeous bodies. I could see their hands moving as they slowly began to explore each other right there in front of me. My cock was so hard that it felt like it would burst at any moment. I am not really sure how long I had watched, but I was now ready to join them.

They were both panting for air as I brought them onto the bed. They both again began kissing me and now their hands were exploring all over my body. It was thrilling to feel four hands touching me all over. Two mouths kissing me and four breasts brushing back and forth across my chest as they took little opportunities to again kiss each other. I had obviously opened a door for them that they had been desiring for quite some time.

The next time that they paused for a long passionate kiss with each other, I scooted out from between them and pressed them together so they fell in each other's arms with Susan on top of Amy. "Why don't you show Amy how much you want to make love to her?" I said it very softly in Susan's ear.

I rolled away and very slowly stroked my cock as I watched Susan do what she has wanted to do for a very long time. She kissed Amy very tenderly then lifted her face. "I have loved you since grade school," she whispered lovingly. "I have wanted this as long as I can remember!" She bent her head down and began to gently kiss her best friend's breasts. "Oooh Suzy....Suzy, me too...I've wanted this too," Amy moaned her reply.

My cock was oozing so much precum as I watched them that it became slicker and slicker as I continued to masturbate. It was electrifying to witness their lust for one another and to watch how greedily they touched and probed and explored each other. My dick was aching by the time that Susan made her way between Amy's legs and began to eat her pussy. "Oh yes, Suzy...Oh my God I've wanted this," Amy moaned lustily.

I don't think they even noticed when I got off the bed and repositioned the camera hidden in the corner. I adjusted it for a closer angle then made my way back behind Susan who was on her knees. "Oooh fuck yesss...Fuck me, Connor. Fuck me!" Susan's bellowed.

Slap, slap, slap, slap... my belly smacked against Susan's ass cheeks as I pounded into her savagely. Amy had both hands on Susan's head and was grinding her hungry cunt into her face. Suddenly Amy began to moan very loudly. It almost sounded like an animalistic growl as her hips began to jerk violently into Susan's face. "I'm cumming. I'm cumming, baby. I'm cumming," she screamed.

As Amy thrashed and wiggled beneath us, I felt a sudden gush of fluid as Susan was reaching her orgasm too. The sensation of her best friend cumming in her face and the gush of fluids that were now streaming into her mouth sent her over the edge. "Oh my God, yes. Ooooh yes. Oooh yes!" Susan moaned her orgasmic reply. My cock exploded into Susan's hot sloppy hole flooding her with my semen until it was oozing out onto her thighs.

As we laid there and rested, they both kissed me repeatedly and thanked me for helping them to satisfy that secret desire that they had both wanted for so long. After we repeated the session with me fucking Amy as she ate Susan's pussy, we all fell asleep together. It was wonderful to watch them all snuggled up and spooned together. About 3 a.m., I quietly got out of bed, fetched my video camera and left them a short note before I left to go home to my apartment.

Girls:

Tonight really was a special night for all of us! I will never forget how wonderful this was... Ever! The room is rented until Monday... Feel free to make use of it as long as you like!!

Hugs...
Connor

IT WAS just after noon when I got out of bed for the second time that Saturday. As I threw open the curtains in my apartment, I saw it was a bright sunny day and there was a young woman laying on one of the lounge chairs out by the pool. She was wearing a tiny white bikini. My mind instantly thought of Mandy and I felt my dick immediately begin to swell as I remembered her naked body out in the cabana at home.

I felt a slight sense of bewilderment as my cock swelled to full erection. Last night had been the only night in the six weeks that I have been back at college that I had not thought of her. It was the only night that I had not needed to masturbate to get her out of my mind long enough to be able to go to sleep. At first, I had thought that this was some perverse desire to get even with my father for all the years of humiliation. But now, I realize that it is much deeper than that. She is much more important to me than that somehow.

I felt a growing knot in my stomach that day as I masturbated in the shower and thought of her superbly soft tanned body with the lily white triangles. I moaned her name out loud as I spewed my seed all over the shower wall. *"I must get her out of my mind somehow!"* I thought to myself.

As I dried off, I reasoned within myself that I had better make some sort of plan to deal with this by the time I return home.

Chapter Three

My father did not show up for my graduation ceremony. He sent Mandy instead with the news that he had to go to Paris for two weeks on some sort of merger deal. "You know he wanted to be here!" she tried to defend him. I could tell by the look on her face that she knew that was a lie. I did not hide my contempt from her. "I don't think we should lie to each other anymore," I stated it calmly but I could tell that she could hear a bit of temper in my voice.

"You're right, he's an asshole...he should have been here!" her hand reached forward and gently touched my arm.

I escorted Mandy to the spectator bleachers and left her there to go down my cap and gown for the ceremony. From my seat on the graduation platform, I could easily see her even buried in the huge crowd around her. As the endless names were called one by one, my eyes seemed to constantly wander back to her. She had her eyes glued to me each time I glanced over at her. It took every particle of my self-control to not get a boner right there on that stage platform. I would never be able to live down the humiliation of having an erection when my name was called.

Mandy was waiting for me by the bleachers after the ceremony. Although she had dressed more conservatively than she usually does, she was still the sexiest woman I had ever seen. She was wearing a pair of those very tight "skinny jeans" and a very tight fitting cashmere sweater with a plunging neck that was short so you could see her belly from just above her navel. With her voluptuous figure she was stunning. Her waist-length platinum blond hair was pulled into a ponytail. I noticed lots of wishful glances by the guys filing by as she bent forward and kissed me on the cheek.

"I'm going to need a ride to the hotel," she whispered into my ear as she kissed me. "I took a taxi straight here from the airport." As I glanced at the very small duffel bag she had at her feet

I grinned sheepishly. "Oooh...I thought that was just a large purse," I chuckled. But I really HAD thought it was just a purse.

As we pulled out of the parking garage, I suggested that we go have dinner before I took her to the hotel. It had been a long graduation ceremony and with her 3-hour flight here I knew she must be hungry. "I'd like that," she replied. "It could be sort of like...a date!" she had a coy little grin as I glanced over at her. As she leaned forward to adjust her stiletto heels, I got a terrific look down her loose top at her gorgeous jugs. "Ooh God!" I whispered. She turned her head towards me and giggled as she saw the growing lump in my 501 jeans.

We went to one of those nationwide type of restaurants that was on the hub between the airport and the hotel where she was staying. We sat in a booth in the back corner where it was fairly quiet and sort of private. I was surprised when she chose to sit on the padded bench next to me rather than the one across from me. After the waiter left after providing the menus and taking our beverage order, she leaned over and kissed me again on the cheek. "I just wanted to be close...so we can talk without others hearing us," she whispered into my ear.

We mostly did chit chat sort of conversation until the waiter came back to take our meal order. Mandy took the time to catch me up on Dad's busy schedule. I noticed that he left very little time to include her in any of his activities. In the past two months she had been taken out only twice to political fund raising parties. And then, it appeared that she was only there as his arm candy.

The rest of this time she has mostly been alone at the Estate with the exception of her twice weekly pilates sessions. She even confided that she has been so bored that she had considered trying to seduce her female pilates instructor. She said it in a joking manner, but I could tell by the look in her eyes that she really had considered it.

As we were eating our meal, she moved her right leg over so her foot was between my two feet and her leg was brushed up against the inside of my left leg. She left it there for most of the time we were eating. It felt sort of strange to me at first. She was not moving her foot or trying to do anything sexual like that one time at home. Then it occurred to me that this was a sort of intimacy. That she was trying to feel connected somehow.

Throughout the dinner, each time she bent forward even just a little, I was able to see straight down her top. Although I tried not to look, I just could not keep my eyes off her wonderful tits. My cock was pounding painfully in my tight 501 jeans by the time the waiter removed the dishes and left the dinner tab. Mandy had leaned forward holding her coffee cup in both hands with elbows resting on the table. I could clearly see all of both her breasts.

When I glanced up from a long look down her top, she was staring at me with a silly grin on her face. "It's OK if you look at them, Connor." It was a soft inviting whisper. "I like how your face looks when you look at me," she informed me. "And I LOVE how it affects you!" Her eyes looked down at the lump in my pants. She reached over a gently petted it for a moment. "It makes me feel like I'm still sexy!"

My entire body was trembling as she withdrew her hand from my lap. "Are you kidding me!" I gasped. "You are so fucking gorgeous. I'm sure that Dad...?" She lifted a finger to my lips to stop my words. "Your father doesn't desire anyone...he only uses them!" It was a shock to hear those words come out of her mouth. "The only time he desires me is...after...." Her voice stopped in mid-sentence and she suddenly had a petrified look of fear on her face. "Maybe we should leave now," she whispered so soft I nearly couldn't hear her request.

On the short five-minute drive to the hotel, she was absolutely silent. Her face was pointed straightforward and I could see that her body was slightly rocking forward and back. Like people often do when they are extremely worried or upset in some way. My heart felt so sad for this gorgeous young woman. What could be so terrible to cause her so much pain? I could not possibly envision how anyone would ever want to cause her this much grief.

"You should come up with me," her voice was trembling as I parked the car. "We need to talk to finish this." She glanced over at me. "I need you to understand, Connor." Her hand was cold and shaking as she placed it on top of mine. "I need you to understand!" she said with conviction.

Mandy had rented the Penthouse Suite of the nearest airport hotel. It was the sort of room that my father would book for his business travels. There was a large living room, a small but fully stocked kitchen with a wet bar, two bedrooms and a huge bathroom which included a hot tub Jacuzzi. The master bedroom had a king-size bed in it and had a balcony that looked out over the river towards the airport. The second bedroom was smaller and had a queen-size bed.

As soon as we were in the door, Mandy made a beeline to the bar. "I need a drink!" her voice sounded anxious and fearful. I watched her pour a 4oz tumbler full of Cognac and down it in one huge gulp. Then she poured a second one then filled a second tumbler for me. I saw her body shudder as she belted down that first drink. I saw her take a deep breath as she turned to me holding a tumbler in each hand. It appeared that she was beginning to relax. "I don't...usually drink," she whispered apologetically.

After she handed me my drink, she gently took my hand and led me to the couch. I could feel that the shaking had ceased and I could tell that she was much more relaxed than I had seen her since we first met. When we sat down, she placed both of her legs on top of mine and sort of leaned against me. "Where to begin?" she whispered as she kicked off her heels. I noticed that she had popped open the first button on her tight jeans before she sat down. She took a quick gulp from her drink, about half of the four ounces, then sat the tumbler on the coffee table.

Over the next half hour, she told me about her relationship with my father. She told me that at first when they were dating, just after he hired her, that he was sweet and attentive to her. She confided that he lavished her with flowers and gifts and special trips that overwhelmed this sweet young girl from Kansas.

She said that she was so smitten with him that she was willing to fulfill his kinky sexual needs in order to repay his kindness and attention. She spoke of bondage and rough sex. She told me that he had difficulty getting an erection unless she pretended that he was forcing her. She confided that he often video recorded their sex encounters so he could watch the videos when he went away alone on business.

There were tears beginning to run down her face as she reached over for the rest of her drink. She swilled it down in one gulp and her body again shuddered as she returned the glass to the table. "The rest is terribly horrific!" her voice quivered as she said it and huge tears welled up in her eyes. "I didn't want to marry him. I didn't want that!" she buried her face in my chest and sobbed uncontrollably for several minutes.

When she finally composed herself enough to continue, she was beginning to slur her words a little. But the cognac gave her the courage to continue. She told me that he had blackmailed her into marrying him by threatening to post their sex tapes online. He had always been very careful to wear a mask as she pretended he was forcing her. He had always used objects to make her climax so it looked like she enjoyed it.

On their wedding night, just after they arrived at the honeymoon suite, four masked men had come out of the second bedroom totally naked except for the masks. My father had told her that this was the only way he could consummate their marriage with her.

They had taken her to the bed, slowly ripped off her wedding gown and then took turns fucking her for several hours. It was not until they left that my father had finally climbed on top of her and consummated the marriage. In the morning, there was a brand new

Mercedes SUV waiting for her in the parking lot. He had told her it was her payment for being his whore.

By now, she was having difficulty keeping her sentences together as the alcohol was beginning to overwhelm her mind and body. The last bit she was able to tell me before she finally passed out, was about her present circumstance. In a mumble, she told me that since the marriage, he has had great difficulties getting erections. She told me the only way he is able to fuck her is after watching other men ravage her. She confided that the forcefulness and pain has escalated a lot over the last six months.

She was now out cold laying against my left side. I thought about carrying her to the master bedroom but decided it best to lay her out on the couch. This way I could put her on her side and the backrest would keep her that way in case she vomited in her sleep. I carefully stretched her out on her side and removed her jeans.

I paused for a moment to gaze at her beautiful young body. But this time I did not get an erection. I was so angry inside about the pain she had been subjected to, that my heart was filled with love for her. I tenderly covered her with a blanket from the bed and kissed her on the forehead. "I will fix this!" I whispered to her.

It was just after midnight when I went into the master bedroom and went to bed. I tossed and turned for hours as I replayed her confession in my mind over and over. I wavered back and forth between feelings of fierce anger followed by overwhelming sadness.

Before I was finally tired enough to fall asleep, I wept for quite some time. It was probably past 3 a.m. when I was finally so exhausted by this rollercoaster of emotion that I finally fell into a fitful sleep.

It was nearly noon when I woke up the next morning. I was greatly surprised to find Mandy in bed with me and spooned up against me from behind. As I tried to gently pull away from her, she grasped me harder with her left arm that was draped over my side. "Don't go. I feel so safe with you," she whispered it in my ear. Then I felt her luscious pouty lips pressed against the back of my neck and she gave me several tender kisses.

My cock was painfully erect because I needed desperately to go take a pee. "I have to pee."

My voice trembled as I said it. Mandy only agreed to let me use the bathroom after I promised her that I would come back and cuddle with her some more afterward. "Oooh. Look at that!" she said with a giggle. Her eyes were glued to my throbbing 9-inch prick that was sticking straight out of the front hole of my boxer shorts. It felt good that she at least had something to giggle about. But I was now very self-conscious about being so exposed to her.

I HAD just finished peeing when Mandy came into the bathroom behind me totally nude. "I changed my mind!" she giggled. Her eyes were glued to my still rigid prick. She filled a cup with some mouth wash and gargled for a few moments then spit it into the sink. "I'd like you to help me in the shower," she sort of whispered it as she bent over to turn on the shower water. The sight of her lily white ass bent over was electrifying to me. I was now pounding hard as she stood back up. "I still feel a little wobbly," she offered as an excuse.

"I don't think this is a good idea," I mumbled my weak reply. But the way my cock was bouncing against my stomach told her an entirely different story. I was relieved to see that wonderful gleam in her eyes that I am used to seeing. I still felt a knot in my stomach as I stepped into the shower with her. Not so much because she is my father's wife. It was more that I desperately wanted this and felt guilty about that desperateness. I was concerned that maybe I was taking advantage of her in a vulnerable moment.

As soon as I turned towards her, Mandy reached out and pulled me towards her until my body was pressed firmly against hers. My cock was mashed up against her lower belly as she wrapped her arms around me with her hands pressed against my upper back. "I've wanted this since the day we met," she whispered it as she kissed my chest by my left shoulder. "I have thought about your hands on my body since that day with the baby oil." Her hands slid down to my ass and she pulled me harder against her. My cock was throbbing against her smooth flat belly.

"At first, it was because I wanted to get even with your father," she whispered it softly into my ear and then very tenderly kissed my neck just inches below my ear. My hands slowly slid down the soft curve of her sides. The sensation of her soft wet skin felt so wonderful. "And then I wanted you because of the desire I saw on your face." she whispered again.

I had just begun to fondle her delicious round ass when I realized that she was sucking a hickey on my neck. "But NOW...I want you to be mine!" she said it plainly and with conviction. She had just slid her hand between us and was fondling my pulsating dick. "I want to be yours, Connor. I want to be yours!" She craned her head up and began to kiss me passionately. As I kissed her back, I could feel the months of secret bottled up lust resonating between us.

Without a second thought I grabbed both her ass cheeks and lifted her up till my hard cock slid between her legs. "Oooh yes, Connor. Fuck me. Please fuck me," she gasped as the head of my prick began to penetrate her dripping pussy lips. My entire body was vibrating as I felt each inch of my prick slip into her hot slippery sexhole. "Oh my god yes," she moaned lustily when I was finally buried to the root.

With her buried on my dick, her wonderful cones with the white triangles were right in my face. I slowly lifted her and dropped her over and over while I sucked greedily on her tits. I had fantasized about these tits every day for two months.

Her hands were wrapped around my head and she was pressing my face harder and harder as I sucked on one nipple and then the other. "Yes, Connor...Take me...Take me," she sighed in a wonderfully throaty voice. I turned slightly so I could press her against the shower wall. I lifted my head and kissed her more passionately than I have ever kissed anyone before.

Thump, thump, thump, thump....her ass smashed against the wall as I pounded into her, fucking her more hungrily and more desperately than I have ever experienced. As I gazed at her face I saw the most contented look of rapture that I had ever seen. Her legs were squeezed around my waist as if she were pulling my cock inside of her as far as she could get it. As I glanced down again at her beautiful young body, I was overwhelmed with the reality that I was finally living the fantasy that has filled my every waking moment for the last several months.

As I replayed in my mind her confession about her desire for me, my cock began to ejaculate deep inside of her quivering vagina. "Oooh my god yes," it was a deep husky moan as her body began to jerk against the shower wall. I held my cock buried in her until her tidal wave of orgasm finally subsided.

When I lifted her off my prick and gently set her back down, I had to hold her up as her knees practically buckled. "That was fantastic...you made my knees weak!'" She giggled as I held her tightly in my arms. I was giddy inside from the exquisite pleasure of actually having her in my arms. From the wonderful reality that I had been able to be inside of her. From the unexpected thrill that she has desired me just as deeply and completely as I had her.

We soaped and rubbed and fondled each other for quite some time. We kissed and giggled and frolicked like a couple of infatuated teenagers until the water finally became cold. As I was drying her off from behind with the huge soft towel, I pulled her back into my arms and kissed the back of her neck. "I made you a promise last night after you passed out," I whispered it into her ear before I kissed her again. "I am going to fix this!"

Chapter Four

I had originally planned to make the three day drive home in my 5-year old Mercedes SUV. But now I had other priorities. As I locked up my apartment for the very last time, I waved to the young teen couple that lived across the way.

"My girl and I need a ride to the airport," I told them as they approached. I held up the keys and jingled them. "If you could be good enough to give us a lift...in your new car!" I placed the keys in Bob's hand. "I've already signed the title over to you. It's in the glove box."

Just as the wheels clunked into the wheel bay below us in First Class, Mandy leaned over and kissed me on the cheek. "That was really sweet...what you did for them," she whispered in my ear. I felt her hand reach into my lap. "My pussy is so wet for you right now!" she whispered.

After the stewardess offered us drinks, I reached up and handed her a fifty dollar bill. "Could we get maybe 20 minutes of privacy?" I asked her softly. She smiled coyly and winked as she shoved the bill into her bra. "The captain will come out in about 45 minutes. I'll see to it that you are not disturbed until then!" she replied. After she pulled out a couple of small blankets from the overhead and handed them to me, she smiled again. "Enjoy yourselves!" she giggled.

As soon as she had closed the heavy curtains to the main cabin, I turned to my side and slipped my hand up into Mandy's miniskirt. I was pleased when she spread her legs wide apart for me and even more delighted when I found that her panties were soaking wet. We both lowered the back of our seats and were now facing each other side by side. It thrilled me to feel her pulling each of the buttons open on my 501 jeans.

I raised my ass so she could pull my jeans down enough to expose my throbbing prick. As I pulled her panties away from her dripping gash, she began to slowly stroke my prick. "Oooh yes, Connor. Yes!" Her body shivered slightly as I slid a finger up into her. "Oooh yesss," she cooed. My cock was oozing so much seminal fluid that her hand slipped up and down my prick effortlessly.

I bent my finger up inside of her drenched canal and began to rub up and down against her hard erect clit. "Yes...Yes...Do that. Do that," she moaned softly. Her hand was rapidly jerking up and down now. It felt so incredibly erotic to be masturbating each other in an aircraft at thirty thousand feet. It was especially arousing to me that it was Mandy that I was experiencing this with.

It was only a couple of minutes until I felt her legs vibrating as her waves of orgasm started. I quickly inserted two more fingers and slowly drilled them in and out of her pussy as her body jerked in violent spasms. She let go of my cock to cover her mouth to muffle her moans. When her body went limp, I pulled my fingers out of her and leaned over to kiss her on the cheek.

I was very pleased that I had been able to bring her off right here in First Class. I was just reaching down to pull up my jeans and her hand came over to stop me. She rolled over towards me and rested her head in my lap. "You don't have to.....Oooh my God that feels so good!" The sensation of her hot mouth engulfing my dick was thrilling.

Her head was bouncing up and down very rapidly as if she was hungry for my cock. The drool running out of her mouth oozed down onto my balls and the slurping noises were so erotic that I was very quickly building up for my discharge. "I'm going to cum, baby," I warned her in a very soft moan. I felt her fingers begin to tickle underneath my sloppy wet balls as she sucked me even harder. As my cock began to spit my load of cream into her mouth, she sucked on the head of my prick like it was a straw. She swallowed and swallowed like she was drinking a milkshake. When my legs finally relaxed, she lifted her head and wiped her mouth off. "Yummy!" she giggled softly. I had just got my jeans back up when the stewardess returned.

Mandy drove us home from the airport in her SUV that she had left in the parking garage. As we drove down the freeway, her short mini skirt rode up high enough that I could see that she was no longer wearing panties. "I sure wish I could stick my cock in that," I chuckled as I gazed at her pink slit. Her pussy lips were still slightly swollen from my rubbing on her during the flight home. "As soon as we're home I'm gonna fuck your brains out!" she replied with a smile.

Mandy was true to her word and dragged me to the couch and fucked me right out in the middle of the living room even though the maid, the butler and the cook were all in the house. By now, we have decided to throw all caution to the wind. We have a plan. It actually aroused me beyond belief when I saw the maid at the top of the stairs watching us with a shocked look on her face. I made it a point to bellow out my moan as I emptied my seed deep into Mandy's womb. I also noticed the kitchen door swaying slightly as we got up off the couch. We then walked back to my room in the rear wing totally naked...holding hands.

We spent the afternoon in my bed. We fucked and napped till dinner time. When the butler called to announce dinner, we held hands as we talked downstairs to the dining room. After we were served, we told the butler to dismiss the cook for the night and that he too could retire to his quarters. We waited until we knew that they had left and that we had the house to ourselves. Then we could begin our search. This was critical for our plan.

We scoured the downstairs pool room where the majority of the sex tapes had been filmed. Mandy had confided that she had been taken there on many occasions to entertain his friends. Usually four to six other men took turns fucking her while my father video recorded every moment of it. Since it had been less than a week since the last party, there was a good chance we might find something of interest, something incriminating.

In a trashcan, we found several used condoms. My dad insisted that the men who were not "fixed" must use condoms. He did not want to take the risk of her getting knocked up by any of his rich and influential friends. We found a bevy of wipes with globs of dried semen. We found a sock, one pair of men's bikini briefs and two tripods for the video cameras. I photographed all of it on my SLR camera to upload to my laptop. We also bagged each item and labeled where it was found.

Just as we were about to leave, I noticed several little square things laying underneath the pool table. It turned out to be four Polaroid snapshot photos that someone had dropped. In the first photo, one of the men was crammed between Mandy's legs. Since the photo was taken from behind, it also had a good background shot. In the photo, you could see the dread on Mandy's face while she was being fucked by the masked man. In the background, you could clearly see my father videotaping it while he was jerking off.

In the second photograph, one of the men was jerking off on her tits. In the background there were two men standing next to my father as they watched. They had removed their masks while they were resting. In the third photo, one man was fucking Mandy from behind and had removed his mask so he could breathe easier. In the background you could see his face very clearly in the mirror just behind my father. And now the two men next to him were playing with each other as they watched the man fucking Mandy.

The final photo would prove to be the one I would most cherish throwing in my father's face. While one of the men was on top of Mandy fucking her, another one was humping her mouth.

In the background, there was a man on his knees sucking my father off while he videotaped his wife being ravaged. The man was not wearing a mask. I could easily see that he was Dad's oldest friend, Senator Bilbee.

I could see that Mandy was visibly shaken by the evidence we had found. I could see the deep shame in her face as I had glanced at the four photographs. She was trembling when I pulled her into my arms and kissed her gently on the forehead. "You must think I am such a whore!" she whispered. "Not in a million years," I replied as I lifted her chin with one of my fingers. "This only proves what a sick fuck my father is and all of his buddies too!" My voice was now full of rage.

I pulled her against my chest and let her cry it out. When she finally settled down, I again lifted her chin and kissed her tenderly. "You will never have to do that again. I promise!" I whispered. I held up the photos. "This...is what will make that possible!" I reminded her. I held her hand as we slowly walked to the upstairs wing of the Estate. That is where Father's private library is. That is where we will most likely find his secret videos hidden.

Mandy had tried on many occasions to locate the videos but has never been able to get into his library. He keeps it locked up tighter than a drum anytime he is not in it himself. Fortunately, many years ago when I was a child, I accidentally found where he hides his extra key. There are little tables with vases of flowers all along the hallway leading to his library. They all have little drawers in them. They are all empty. If you pull the drawer out of the very last table next to the doorway to his office, the key is taped on the underside of the drawer.

Mandy was a little antsy as I turned the key in the lock. "I know this is difficult, baby, but it is our freedom...for good!" I whispered as we entered the library. As I glanced around his private study, I racked my memories of all the secret hiding places I had discovered as a very nosey and very observant child that Dad never paid attention to.

I knew that he would not put video disks in his safe in the wall. The one behind the portrait of his mother that was mounted on hinges. That would be difficult to conceal during business deals that required him to open the safe. I knew it would not be in any of his desk drawers because they would be too easily broken into. Then, I remembered the secret room behind the center of wall of books. The room I found when I was thirteen. The room that had liquor, nasty films and girly magazines inside. I also remembered exactly which book to move to find the secret lever.

"This is horribly disgusting!" Mandy gasped softly as we glanced around the 20-foot square secluded room. There was a small single bed in one corner that had obvious cum stains all over it. There were many extremely hard core sex magazines stacked next to a desk with a laptop. There was a trash bucket in the corner next to the desk flooding over with waded tissues of dried semen. There were greasy smudges all over the desk and laptop. There were several different types of tubes of lubricant next to the laptop and more on the floor next to the bed.

"What a sick son-of-a-bitch!" I gasped. Against the opposite wall from the bed, there was a half dozen file type boxes stacked up. Next to that was a table with several video cameras. We also noticed that there was a hole drilled in the wall that would allow him to make secret videos of inside the library from inside his sex room.

When I glanced through the six boxes, I found the videos. Thirty five years of videos. Many of the older ones were obviously DVD copies of what were once probably VCR tapes. "We'll never be able to copy ALL of these," I whispered. We were both stunned at the absolute depravity of this man we thought we knew.

We managed to locate all of the recordings of Mandy. Fortunately, my father is meticulous about labeling and organizing things. There were eighteen of them which meant Mandy had been subjected to this once per month since her wedding night when it all began. I could see the tears welling up in her eyes as she understood that I had made that connection.

"It's OK, baby. It will all be over soon!" I kissed her again tenderly to let her know that I did not hold her responsible for any of this.

As I rifled through the other five boxes, I noticed the names of all the different maids that he has hired over the years. All of his secretaries, all of his personal assistants and most of his friends' wives. I pulled about a dozen of them out to add to the ones of Mandy. I was just about to close the last box when something caught my eye. It was my mother's name and their wedding date. I suddenly felt sick to my stomach as I pulled it out of the box. On the very next disc behind that one, was her sister's name...and the same date. I grabbed that one too.

Mandy was so upset that evening that I had to give her a sleeping pill to get asleep. As soon as she was out cold, I started the process of recording bits and pieces of each of the sex tapes to keep for ourselves as evidence. I was glad she was out cold as I sorted through each of the 18 recordings. I did my best to focus on all the background shots and close ups of anybody markings that would identify the men in the room. But it tore my heart out every time I let down my guard and remembered it was her that was being used by these men.

Mandy had confided that she had gone along with it at first as just some sort of sex game that would make my father happy with her. Then, as he paid her with gifts each time, she truly began to feel like she was the whore that he said she was. She had wanted it to stop, but he reminded her that the recordings would make it impossible for any man to ever want her again.

The sun was just coming up when I finally got to the last two videos. By the time I had watched all of the sick and depraved things that he had done with his maids and secretaries, I had a knot in my stomach as I started the video of my mother. I was on my knees puking when Mandy woke up. Each time I glanced up at my laptop, I would vomit again and again.

My father had slowly removed her wedding gown and then laid her on the bed. After removing her bra and panties, he had blindfolded her and then tied her hands and feet to the bed posts. Just like he did with Mandy. After he had her all tied up, he stripped naked and then walked over to the door that opened into the next hotel room and then stepped into the other room.

Moments later, another man stepped back into the room. He was naked. I watched in horror as he crawled on top of my mother and began to fuck her. The man was Senator Bilbee. When I watched the last video, it was of my father fucking my mother's sister who was also blindfolded and all tied up. They were doing this at the same moment in time. It was Mandy that reached over and shut off the recording equipment and saved it all to the flash disc.

Although I had managed to find a trash bucket to puke into, I needed a shower. I had never felt so filthy in my entire life. It felt like my skin wanted to crawl off of me. Mandy just stood there and we held each other in the steaming hot shower spray. We stood there and sobbed until the all the hot water ran out. As soon as I dried off, I quickly went back to the secret room in the library and returned all the videos to their proper places. I was just on the way to my room when the butler arrived.

I finally crawled into bed for some much needed sleep. Mandy crawled in behind me and just cuddled with me. I was so exhausted that I fell into a deep but fitful sleep. When I awoke, it was just past 2 pm. Mandy was sleeping gently but woke up too as soon as she felt me move. "We don't have to do this today," I whispered as I rolled towards her. I was referring to the plan we had set in motion yesterday when we fucked in front of the maid.

My father had warned me long ago to never do anything too frisky on the outside grounds of the estate. He informed me that the paparazzi have often set up high powered cameras to try to film something provocative to embarrass him with. He had also told me that he suspected that Lanna, our maid, was the one that would call them with information.

When we screwed in front of her yesterday, we were sure she would notify her contact that there was something that he would be interested in. When we threw open the drapes, we could see a glint of bright light in the tall tree at the other end of the estate. It was the sun gleaming off of a camera lens.

"I need to do this now!" Mandy whispered her reply. She opened the window so the photo would clearly show she was naked in my room. "Let's give them a show they will never forget!" I could hear the determination in her voice.

It was a quarter till three when Mandy and I went out to the pool. We had watched the man climbing back up into the tree after he had taken a break of some sorts. Through the binoculars I also noticed that he had a huge telephoto lens on his SLR type camera. This meant that he would easily be able to zoom in on the show we were about to give him.

I started by applying tanning oil all over Mandy's body, making sure he had plenty of shot of my hands wandering inside of her bikini top and also into her bottoms. We then laid in the sun for about fifteen minutes. I took several opportunities to reach over and fondle her firm little ass. I glanced up at the house each time as if I was checking to see if it was safe to fondle her.

Next, we got onto the pool and frolicked for a little while. Kissing and fondling and splashing water all around. I was certain that our secret cameraman enjoyed the fact that Mandy's white bikini top was virtually transparent when it was wet. We made our way to the far end of the pool where he would get a much closer view of us. I pulled her top open and began greedily sucking on her tits while I pulled the strings loose so her top floated away. By the way that Mandy was trembling. I could tell that she was getting aroused.

After five minutes of my hungry attack on her breasts, Mandy suddenly pulled herself out of the pool and ran topless to the cabana that was nearest to that end of the pool. The doorway faced away from main house but directly towards the cameraman. He would have a perfect view of us from his perch in the tree.

I waited for a few moments and then made a quick dash to the cabana as if I was trying to not be seen from the house. Mandy met me at the doorway and we kissed passionately as I let my hands roam all over her now naked body. Mandy slowly kissed her way down my body till she was on her knees.

I turned and leaned against the door frame as Mandy pulled my swim trunks to my ankles, exposing my fully erect 9-inch prick. From his angle, the cameraman had a terrific side view as Mandy engulfed my entire dick with her hot drooling mouth.

Gluck, gluck, gluck, gluck. Mandy gagged a little each time the head of my dick rammed into her throat. As she gagged, large strands of saliva gushed out of her mouth and ran down onto her chest. Within a few minutes her chest and breasts were completely covered with the slimy gooey mess. I reached down and lifted her to her feet.

After kicking off my swim trunks, I carried Mandy to the changing bench and lowered her back onto her feet. I then laid down on the bench directly in front of the open doorway and Mandy stepped over me to straddle my throbbing hard-on. Mandy was so aroused that her pussy was dripping down onto my thighs as she squatted over me.

"Oooh, Baby...you feel so good," Mandy moaned softly as she slowly lowered herself till she was impaled on my prick. This would also be a side view for the cameraman which was important so that both our faces could be identified.

"Fuck me, sweetie. Fuck me!" I gasped as she began to rock back and forth on my cock. I reached up and gently twisted both of her nipples until they were as hard as little stones.

After about five minutes of very slowly lifting up and sliding back down on my prick so the cameraman would get some close-ups of my dick penetrating her, Mandy stood up and had me sit on the bench so she could face the camera.

"I want that bastard to see how much I enjoy fucking you," she whispered as she guided my dick back into her gash.

Smack, smack, smack, smack...she was now humping me furiously. The sound of her ass slamming down against my thighs echoed through the tiny cabana. "NOW, BABY. I'M CUMMING NOW!" I screamed as I felt the load racing to the head of my dick.

Mandy quickly rose up off my cock just as I began to ejaculate. With my dick right between her thighs, she reached down and jerked me off so my cum sprayed all over her lower belly. When my dick finally stopped spewing, she giggled as she used her free hand to smear my semen all over her tits. "That should get his attention!" She laughed wickedly.

Chapter Five

Robert was sitting outside on the balcony patio of his French chateau just west of Paris. He was sipping at his morning coffee while Evonne, his mistress of the last nine years, was taking a shower. It was a brilliant warm sunny morning as he enjoyed the fresh morning breeze. Even though the first hints of autumn were in the air, it was still warm enough that he had just fucked his paramour right here on the table in front of him.

After he sat his coffee on the table, Robert turned his attention to the envelope that had just arrived moments ago by special delivery. There was a large heavy brown sealed envelope and a newspaper of some sort that was tied on top. Robert untied the string so he could unfold the paper and see the front page. It was one of those rag newspapers that specialize in the type of stories that the paparazzi love to sensationalize.

Robert felt like the structure he was gazing at seemed familiar as he took a sip of his coffee.

Suddenly, the coffee was spraying forcefully from his mouth as he recognised the two faces in the photograph. "YOU FUCKING WHORE!" he screamed after spraying his coffee out of his mouth.

He quickly reached down and grabbed the envelope and ripped the top off of it in one fast motion. He reached inside and pulled out about a dozen 8 by 10 glossy photos that had a short handwritten note by the owner of the newspaper. "I have hundreds more of these if you'd care to provide comment...for clarity. Call me!"

In the first couple of photos, his son was spreading oil on his wife and obviously feeling her tits and pussy. In the next couple, they were in the pool and his son was sucking his wife's tits. In the third bunch of photos, Mandy was on her knees sucking Connor's cock. Then there were a bunch of them fucking on the bench. In the final photo, Mandy was facing the camera and smearing Connor's semen all over her breasts. She had a wicked look on her face and it almost appeared like she was looking directly into the camera lens.

Robert had slumped in his chair. For a moment, the tightness in his chest almost felt like he was going to have a heart attack. Robert had never had anyone defy him like this in his entire life. He has always been the one in control. He has always been the one with the upper hand and the money to do as he pleased. "YOU FUCKING CUNT!" he screamed as he threw the photos onto the table. Within an hour, Robert had booked a flight home from Paris.

"YES, SIR...Yes, Sir. Right away, Sir!" You could see Charles the butler cowering as he talked with Robert on the phone. "I'll dispatch the limo right away, Sir!" You could see Charles shaking as he listened to the instructions. "No, Sir...Not a word...Not a word!" Charles glared at us when he saw us smiling as he hung up the phone.

"HOW COULD YOU!" He shouted at us. Mandy stepped in front of him to block his escape.

"You HAD to know what was happening to me at those special parties downstairs!" Mandy was poking Charles in the chest with a finger. "How could YOU keep his secret?" she shouted right back at him.

"That would be disc number 387!" I offered as a reason for his silence. Charles had been caught with Pete, the cook, in a sexual encounter with each other in the kitchen. They had thought that it would be fun and safe since there was no one at home that evening. They had never expected that Robert had set up a hidden video camera.

The following two discs were of each of them being called into Robert's library to face their indiscretion. After Robert explained the conditions of his silence, he had made each of them suck him off if they wanted to keep their jobs. They have both been at his mercy for over ten years. They have both had to look the other way concerning many horrid perversions of their blackmailing employer.

After we promised that Robert would never know that we had talked, Charles confided that

Robert would be home within the hour. "He will never guess that we talked," I assured him. "Not after he sees what we are doing when he finds us!" Mandy giggled softly. Charles then rushed off quickly to be sure that the house was in proper order.

Mandy and I had heard his limo pull up downstairs. We were waiting for him together in my bed...naked. I had a large brown envelope laying on the bed next to me. Mandy was curled up on the other side of me. She was casually sucking my cock as we heard his footsteps coming up the back staircase to my room.

My father froze in his footsteps once he flung open my door. There was a momentary silence as his eyes focused on the fact that we were nude and that Mandy was sucking my dick. She did not bother to stop. The pleasure of her greedy mouth sucking me off right in front of him was deliciously spectacular. "That feels wonderful, sweetheart!" I said it loud enough to break through his frozen trance.

"Aaaaah...YOU FUCKING WHORE!" Dad was now moving towards the bed. He had a large brown envelope under his arm and a newspaper of some sorts.

"I may be a whore...but not yours anymore!" Mandy had lifted her head to spit the words at him, the drool from her mouth oozed down onto her tits. He stopped in his tracks right next to the bed as I lifted my brown envelope.

"I'll show you mine if you show me yours!" I laughed at him. "Although, I already know what is in your package!" I laughed again as I poured the contents of the envelope out onto the bed.

Mandy went back to sucking my prick as I spread out the photos so he could clearly see what was on them. "These are of your sick little secret sex room upstairs. Notice all the cum filled wipes!" Then I told him that we have collected some of them in an evidence bag. "Notice all those boxes against the wall," I smiled at him. "Imagine what we found inside all those boxes?"

I loved it that Mandy was making loud slurping noises. "That feels so good, baby!" I saw the grimace on his face as he continued to look through the photographs. "These, here, are of the basement where you had that little fuck fest last week." I tossed them closer so he could see them better. "Notice all the bags of evidence!" Then I pointed out all the used condoms, wipes and then the Polaroid photos. I could see his hands were trembling as he held the photos up.

I was thrilled that Mandy was giving me head the entire time that I was doing to him the same thing he has done to so many others. "And these..." I pushed the two DVD's I had recorded over to him. "These are bits and pieces of the last thirty years!" As he lifted them from the bed, his hands were visibly shaking uncontrollably.

As he stood there with a look of horror on his face, I explained to him that I had carefully edited each little video. I told him how I had focused on background faces, body markings and many other things that I noticed that could identify all of his playmates. I could feel myself getting close to climax as I held up the last item that I wanted him to see.

"But this is my favorite shot of all!" I handed him the photo of Senator Bilbee sucking his cock in the room downstairs. "YES BABY...NOW, BABY...NOW, BABY!" as my father's face became ashen and full of panic. Mandy yanked my dick out of her mouth and my three wads of semen sprayed all over her face and tits. "Ooooh...I love how you do that!" I moaned. Dad suddenly bent over and puked all over the floor. "What do you want?" he groaned softly, submissively.

Mandy and I explained the details of the divorce to him. He could use the infidelity that we had so carefully staged as his way to save face. Mandy would keep ALL of the gifts that he had so cruelly used to manipulate her into believing she was his whore. Despite his prenuptial that he had made her agree to, he would give her the beach front condo that has been his secret little sex nest for the last ten years, her Mercedes SUV and he would agree to never contact her in anyway...ever again.

I made it clear that I did not want anything from him. I leaned over and kissed Mandy gently on the cheek. "You already gave me the best gift there is!" I bent forward to kiss her breast. Before he left us, I gave him all of the contents of the envelope. "You can keep these copies for you own enjoyment," I taunted him. "The masters are in a safe deposit box!"

As we pulled away from the estate in Mandy's Mercedes, there was a van pulling onto the property. Charles and Pete were out front holding hands. They had both quit and the van was there to pick up their belongings. They waved to us as we drove past them. Charles held up the three DVD's I had given him that Robert used to blackmail them with. They would come work for us as soon as we found a home of our own. Until then...the condo would be our first taste of freedom. As soon as we removed all the hidden video cameras.

The End

Here is a sample from another story you may enjoy:

JACK RYDER

TRAILER TRASH
Payback
Sweet Revenge

ADULT EROTIC ROMANCE

WE SPENT most of Saturday watching the movers as they loaded the moving van, hauled our belongings to the trailer and then unloaded the van. That evening, we spent moving all the furniture around until we were happy with where each item was. As I was unpacking a couple of boxes that contained the bed sheets and bath towels, I happened to glance out the bedroom window. I could see a young blond hair woman in the trailer across from me. She was completely naked.

She was staring right at me with a slight grin. I was frozen as she moved closer to the window. From what I could see, she looked to be about maybe 23 years old. Her yellow blond hair was in a ponytail and her small perky tits had a slight upturn that made them deliciously sexy. She gave a little wave and then the blinds came down.

There was a sudden noise behind me and I jumped. "It's just me silly!" Anna laughed as she entered the room. "And what are you thinking about?" she giggled playfully when she saw the lump in my jeans. I could see one of the slats open in the blinds across the way. I could see her fingers pulling it farther down as I stood up. I know that she could easily see the bulge even from twenty feet away. "I was thinking how nice this would feel buried in your sweet pussy!" I lied to Anna.

I reached for Anna and pulled her to the bed. "I want you now...I want to break in our new home," I told her softly as I began to pull her sweat pants down. Before she could complain about the window being wide open, I bent down and began licking up and down her smooth bare slit.

"Oh Yes...Yes...Yesss!" Anna moaned as I pulled her sweat pants completely off.

"The window...the wind...ooooh...my God...Yes." Anna's body shuddered as I drove my cock into her pussy in one brutal thrust. I glanced over and saw the blinds opening slightly as I began to pound into Anna's hot wet gash. I lifted myself up with my arms so my secret audience could see every inch of my prick see sawing in and out Anna. "Take Me...Take me, Dex" Anna gasped.

It thrilled me that I could see her silhouette in her blinds as she watched me banging my wife.

I imagined that she was fingering herself. I could practically see her delicious little tits rising and falling as she masturbated. That thought sent me over the edge. "HERE IT IS BABY...HERE IT IS!" As I began to ejaculate, I pulled my dick out and scooted up so my cum sprayed all over Anna's tits. I could just see her eyes for a moment through the slat. Then she closed it tight.

I felt a little guilty that I had cum so quickly and had not satisfied Anna yet. "We're not done yet baby!" I panted softly. I kissed her tenderly as I smeared the semen all over her tits. "I love how sexy your tits feel with me all over them," I whispered in her ear. I continued to smear it all over while I scooted down and started to lick her pussy again. "Yes Baby...Eat Me...Eat Me," Anna moaned as she began to hump herself up into my face.

My dick was quickly swelling again as I thought about the young girl who had been watching us earlier. I could feel Anna's body thrashing beneath me as I brought her closer to her climax.

"OH YES...FUCK ME, DEX...FUCK ME!" It was that deep husky moan that I love so much. Anna was just beginning to jerk underneath me as I drove into her and fucked her savagely as she screamed my name and convulsed uncontrollably. My dick erupted, spitting three huge wads of semen deep into her womb.

We both laid there panting deeply for air for several minutes. When she finally regained her composure, Anna kissed me gently on the cheek. "That was...sensational," she whispered as I rolled off of her. "I wanted our first....to be...special!" I glanced out our window and saw the light in the other bed room finally go out. I was smiling broadly as Anna kissed me again and assured me that it was very special.

Anna and I spent most of the day Sunday unpacking boxes and putting everything away in our new little home. Although I was very pleased with all of the space we had in the three bedroom trailer, Anna complained continually about it being so much smaller than our old home. Late in the afternoon, Anna suddenly told me that she needed to go for a drive and "take a break". I was happy to have the time alone. I felt it would be a good break for the both of us.

Several minutes after she left, I heard a buzzing noise coming from near the couch in the living room. When I located the noise, I found Anna's cell phone on the end table next to the couch. I hesitated a few moments, struggling whether or not I should peek at the text message she had received. My curiosity finally got the best of me and I opened the message.

"Waiting for you, Baby...Been horny for you all day...I'll be in bed waiting...Naked!"

If you enjoyed this sample then look for **Trailer Trash Payback.**

Also by this Author

About the Author

Jack Ryder LOVES everything there is about sex!

When he is not involved with his "swinger" friends, enjoying a steamy threesome, or being part of a raunchy "gang bang", you can find him on first class planes, trains, and cruise ships. Traveling seems to be the BEST way to finding new and interesting sexmates for him. Sexmates. plural. He lives with the saying "The More, The Merrier!"

He owns a successful business in New York. He writes as a hobby and also as sort of documentation of his mind-blowing sexcapades over the years. He is presently roaming around the streets of Manhattan but can be anywhere in the world too, since he travels often. So, beware! You just might be his next mate.

The most fun thing I enjoy when writing my stories is trying to figure out which is fantasy and which was memory. ENJOY! (Preferably with a friend. *wink*)" -Jack Ryder-

From the Author

If you have any comments, suggestions, or would just like to get a little personal, please feel free to email me at:
jack_ryder@awesomeauthors.org

If you enjoyed any of my books then please share the love and click like on my books in Amazon.

If you write me a review and send me an email I will send you a free book, or many. (Just know that these emails are filtered by my publisher.)

Good news is always welcome.

One Last Thing, For Kindle Readers...

When you turn the page, Kindle will give you the opportunity to rate this book and share your thoughts on Facebook and Twitter. If you enjoyed my writings, would you please take a few seconds to let your friends know about it? Because... when they enjoy they will be grateful to you and so will I.

Thank You!

Jack Ryder
jack_ryder@awesomeauthors.org